In the early hours of September 7, 1838,
Grace Darling, the daughter of the
keeper of the Longstone Lighthouse
on the Farne Islands in England,
saw a ship wrecked on the nearby rocks.

Braving the raging storm, she and her
father set out in the family rowboat
and rescued nine people stranded on the
rocks. However, another rescue took
place that day—this one involved a cat
named Gracie and her kitten.

for James & Christopher

Rachel & Emma

Other books by Ruth Brown:

A DARK, DARK TALE

HOLLY: THE TRUE STORY OF A CAT

IMAGINE

NIGHT-TIME TALE

THE OLD TREE: AN ENVIRONMENTAL TALE

SNAIL TRAIL

TEN SEEDS

First American edition published in 2011 by Andersen Press USA, an imprint of Andersen Press Ltd.
www.andersenpressusa.com

First published in Great Britain in 2010 by Andersen Press Ltd.,
20 Vauxhall Bridge Road, London SW1V 2SA.
Published in Australia by Random House Australia Pty.,
Level 3, 100 Pacific Highway, North Sydney, NSW 2060.
Copyright © Ruth Brown, 2010
Jacket illustrations copyright © Ruth Brown, 2010

Distributed in the United States and Canada by
Lerner Publishing Group, Inc.
241 First Avenue North
Minneapolis, MN 55401 U.S.A.
www.lernerbooks.com

Color separated in Switzerland by Photolitho AG, Zürich.
Printed and bound in Singapore by Tien Wah Press.

Library Cataloging-in-Publication Data available.
ISBN: 978-0-7613-7454-1
2 - TWP - 4/22/11
This book has been printed on acid-free paper

With thanks to the Grace Darling Museum, Bamburgh

GRACIE
THE LIGHTHOUSE CAT

Ruth Brown

ANDERSEN PRESS USA

Outside the storm was raging,
but inside the lighthouse,
Gracie and her kitten were warm
and snug in the cozy parlor.

Gracie was sleepy—but her kitten was not.
When he heard the sound of voices and running
footsteps, he decided to investigate.

Down and down he went,
following the sounds . . .

. . . until he stopped at the front door. The gale-force winds,
the driving rain, and the crashing waves were terrifying.
He turned to run back upstairs, when . . .

CRASH!

The wind caught the door
and slammed it shut, hurling
him out into the storm.

Gracie woke with a jump. She was alone. Where was her kitten? She called to him, but there was no answer.

She searched everywhere, all the way down
to the cellar, but still there was no reply.

Gracie climbed out of the cellar window.
She called and called to her kitten, but
her frantic cries were drowned by the
howling wind. It was hopeless.

Just as she was about
to give up her desperate search,
she saw something. . . .

It was her kitten! Cold, terrified,
and soaking wet, he was clinging to
the slippery rocks.

Gently, Gracie picked him up and clawed her way toward the safety of the lighthouse.

She climbed up the winding staircase,
back to the cozy parlor.

After a saucer of milk,
they snuggled down in their
basket by the fire.
Gracie was sleepy and,
this time, her kitten was too.